My Uncle Is Coming Tomorrow

First published in English by
Greystone Books in 2022

Originally published in Spanish in 2014 as
Mañana viene mi tío by Ediciones Del Eclipse

Text and illustrations copyright © 2022
by Sebastián Santana Camargo

Translation copyright © 2022 by Elisa Amado

22 23 24 25 26   5 4 3 2 1

Greystone Kids / Greystone Books Ltd.
greystonebooks.com

An Aldana Libros book

Cataloguing data available from Library and
Archives Canada

ISBN 978-1-77840-006-3 (cloth)
ISBN 978-1-77840-007-0 (epub)

Original jacket and interior design by the author

The illustrations in this book were rendered in
Photoshop.

Printed and bound in Canada on FSC® certified
paper at Friesens. The FSC® label means that
materials used for the product have been responsibly
sourced.

Greystone Books gratefully acknowledges the
Musqueam, Squamish, and Tsleil-Waututh peoples on
whose land our Vancouver head office is located.

Greystone Books thanks the Canada Council for the
Arts, the British Columbia Arts Council, the Province
of British Columbia through the Book Publishing Tax
Credit, and the Government of Canada for supporting
our publishing activities.

Canadä

Sebastián Santana Camargo
Translated by Elisa Amado

My Uncle
Is Coming
Tomorrow

AN ALDANA LIBROS BOOK

GREYSTONE KIDS

GREYSTONE BOOKS • VANCOUVER / BERKELEY / LONDON

My father and mother told me that my uncle is coming tomorrow to stay with us for a few days.

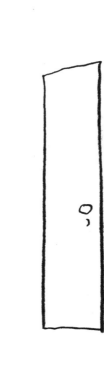

Great! Then I can ask him how to stop a penalty shot.

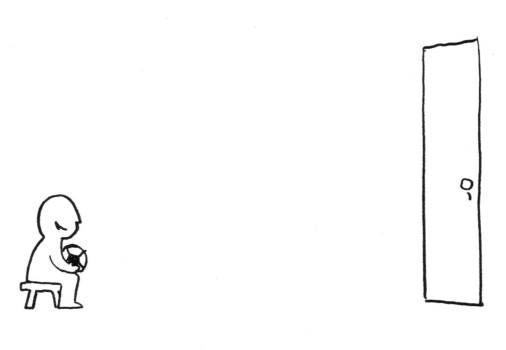

Great! Then I can show him how I've been doing in school.

Great! Then I can tell him about this girl that I like.

Great! Then he can help me to move.

Great! Then I can show him my son.

Great! Then we can celebrate the fact that I finally got my degree.

Great! Then he can meet my granddaughter.

Great! Then he can see that I can still walk.

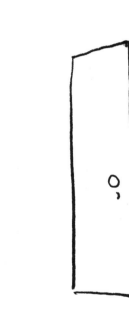

This book is for those who, because of forced disappearances, were never able to come.

Afterword
TO BE DISAPPEARED

Throughout history people have disappeared. Their unexplained absence leaves a searing pain in those left behind. They never know what happened to their loved one, whether it be a father or mother, a son or daughter, or a friend.

But it was only in the middle of the twentieth century, during the Cold War, that "disappearing people" became a systematic instrument of terror used by governments—a way of getting rid of political enemies, of extinguishing their ideas, and of creating such fear that people stopped their political activity. We can assume that these people were murdered. But in the majority of cases their bodies were never found or identified, and their families never knew what had happened to them. Because there was no proof of their loved one's death, people of course waited and waited for them to return. To cause this pain is one of the most terrible things that can be done by one person to another.

An extreme example of this practice took place in 1965, when the Indonesian military, with the help of the United States' Central Intelligence Agency (CIA), overthrew the legitimate government of Indonesia's President Sukarno. They followed up by disappearing somewhere between 500,000 and 3,000,000 people. This came to be known as the "Jakarta Method," and it was successful in moving Indonesia into the US's political and economic orbit.

In the years following World War II, when large numbers of people in countries in South and Central America began to actively seek social and political reforms that threatened local and outside corporate interests, the United States supported dictatorships that had overthrown democratically elected governments. These interventions involved training Latin American military personnel in what was called "counterinsurgency."

CIA officers and US military personnel suggested to local militaries and members of the upper classes that it would be a good idea to look at the effectiveness of the Jakarta Method. So began the terrible period of the Latin American dictatorships that lasted from the 1960s through the mid-1990s, during which hundreds of thousands of people were disappeared. This book is set in South America in that period.

Disappearing people continues to take place all over the world. This practice that has been condemned by the United Nations is being used, right now, to break the will of ethnic groups standing up for their rights in certain countries. Organized crime has also taken up disappearing people, sometimes with the assistance of corrupt officials. In many countries, journalists are targeted.

The forced disappearance of people is a crime against humanity. Let us inform ourselves about where and when this crime is taking place and insist that no child ever again has to wait his or her whole life for an uncle who never comes.

Please see greystonebooks.com/my-uncle-is-coming-tomorrow for the information upon which this piece is based.

Patricia Aldana, Aldana Libros

About the Author

Sebastián Santana Camargo was born in La Plata, Argentina, and now lives in Montevideo, Uruguay. He is a visual artist and graphic designer as well as a book illustrator.

He has been awarded the prize for best art direction for the animated film *AninA* and the 2018 Paul Cézanne Visual Arts Prize given by the Embassy of France in Uruguay. The Spanish edition of *My Uncle Is Coming Tomorrow*, *Mañana viene mi tío*, won the Grand Prize of ALIJA (IBBY Argentina) and ALIJA's prize for the best picture book in 2014.

Elisa Amado is a translator who was born in Guatemala, where more than 200,000 people were killed or disappeared during the Cold War. She emigrated to Canada in 1971.